Spare Parts

SPARE PARTS

PLUS TWO

GAIL SCOTT

COACH HOUSE BOOKS

Published with the assistance of the Canada Council for the Arts and the
Ontario Arts Council.

NATIONAL LIBRARY OF CANADA CATALOGUING IN PUBLICATION

Scott, Gail

      Spare parts plus two / Gail Scott.

ISBN 1-55245-101-1

      I. Title.

PS8587.C623S62 2002   C813'.54   C2002-903271-7
PR9199.3.S35S62 2002

CONTENTS

The Virgin Denotes   7
Or the Unreliability of Adverbs
To Do with Time

Climbing the Coiled Oak   19

Ottawa   37

Withdrawal   51

Tall Cowboys and True   61

Petty Thievery   71

Bottoms Up   81

Notes   91

The Virgin Denotes

Or the Unreliability of Adverbs To Do with Time

'Dream About Writing': I am lying in bed, the sheet folded down
rather sloppily over the mattress. And this was
embarrassing because I was giving a public reading
about passion from the bed – by myself. Reading looking
straight ahead. And the audience was sitting to my left in
three oblique rows of chairs. Looking not at me, on the
right, but also looking straight ahead (from their oblique
angle), as I, lying in bed, read.

Montréal: It's dark. Walking down l'Esplanade-by-the-park, it feels indiscreet spying on the writer I was then. That old angel monument's visible in the distance. Light seeps from the spacious corrugated glass-brick public washroom façade at the end of the walk. Part of a mayor's project for making a Marie-Antoinette hamlet out of Olmsted's mountain. People nod on benches. Cop car drives up. I keep, for the moment, to the residential [referential] side. Briskly, I walk. Toward the cinema with the best popcorn in the city. For a hit of nostalgia: old Cassavetes. Black Orpheus. La Dolce Vita. Past the gorgeous dwellings, former consuls', downgraded to residences of city councillors [one, anti-vice, shot by a limping man in a raccoon coat police called 'a foreigner'], immigrant families, artists. Trying to glimpse between the cracks in the curtains. A youth in a pillbox passes, trotting even faster. Later, spying the youth in the pillbox in the light of the popcorn machine, I see he's the son of the old man who stuck out his tongue as I stared past his wrought-iron fence, attaching an eschatological name to my person. I trot, feeling [retrospectively] like a miso-coated salmon.

It is this '*later*' I want to talk about:

I was a journalist. '*Then.*' Sentencing, over the fear of being poisoned 'in relation to the mother' [as Freud said of paranoia]. Amassing outfits, bylines, accoutrements of success to stave off the threat of a life like hers. Simultaneously executing patterns of conspiracy in my world of small subjects, women, would-be intellectuals, working-class upstarts. Tentatively, I was practicing growing angry at what they were, the information merchants, and who I risked becoming, her ghost. Taking off and trying on protheses in the cheap lights of old department stores.

I dreaded mornings *after*.

Coming into work at a local daily newspaper – my typewriter faced that of a kindly elder court reporter. Thirteen calls this morning, he informed me sadly. Thirteen calls furious at my taunting article on the 'McGill-Français' demo, featuring commerce students carolling O Canada, well back on the sidewalk. Thirteen outraged members of the English community thinking the city belonged to them. I wanted to fuck with their aura, with that which does not strut about with a label describing what it is. All the same, I was writing careful tight phrases, miming information's racket. Those basic hundred words. Censoring the vernacular, words like class, cunnilingus, capitalist; likewise repressed: 'Some Points about the FLQ Manifesto*.' How phrases went together in precise little columns also seemed inhibitively … structuring. I wanted to mock them in sentences like single grins with lips pasted back [Lisa Robertson].

Simultaneously wanting to write phrases that performed Mallarméan gestures.

The context – bathed in the tender backlight of *later* – encouraged it: a first poetry reading, la Nuit de la Poésie against the War Measures Act [the legislator had suspended all civil rights]. Impressing on fresh adolescent spirits in the dark recesses of the Eglise/Théâtre Gésu a link, possibly indelible, between writing and subversion. People spoke at real risk of being imprisoned. The singer Louise Forestier, pregnant, in braids [a nice touch], stood on the stage, patting the baby in her stomach and singing 'Ferme-la et prends ta bière [Shut-up and drink your beer].' While round that old angel monument by the mountain, cops' horses scattered conga players, waterpipes, skinny loiterers. Recently, walking into a tearoom in Montréal's Quartier Latin, I thought I saw those same skinny youth *again*: apparently eating only carrots and smoking something in waterpipes, conjuring in their spareness the empathy and complicity I tendentiously conjugating with *then*. [You still think you're thirty, a lover complained recently]. It is the artist's task, Ernst Bloch states in Utopia, to bring now-time into line or focus with like historical moments when thought's not emptied out, a turning point. When time has lost its thickness. Talent may be only knowing how to grasp a vector when our lives flow along it.

Dear R, who are the age I was … earlier: The air is empty. The grass, where we walked, is empty. And the space across the bay where the Twin Towers stood. Nostalgia for how things were before. Not so great if you care to remember said Nakila at the Brooklyn Women's Salon. Dear R, I say, playing the older writer walking, arms folded over black raincoat, head bent to the side, a writer must (in the sense of surely) know what impetus causes her *to write this way instead of that. Must (surely) be aware of the risk of foregrounding her by her inscription in the system she opposes when she chooses to write not a line but a sentence. I like that you ask: 'What is the writer's responsibility?' Though I want to say: 'Be careful.' Or: 'Risk.' I like that you are interested in narrative as call and response, linked to address. That for you, in your writing, address is not about the is nor the will-be but the could, keeping both narrator and narrative <u>conditional</u>.* (would).

Meanwhile [Memory being the solicitous trollop she is]: Back in that late-seventies pseudo-revolutionary Wonderland, increasingly medially framed as Québécois spaghetti western, due to the crime rates, *meanwhile*, in a two-storey flat high on a Quartier-Latin promontory called Terrasse Saint-Denis, two musicians [one franco, one anglo], two writers [one franco, one anglo], one visual artist [anglo], one guy in a navy beret from the suburbs [franco], read the Surrealist Manifestos and felt latent content mattered, chain-smoking and analyzing our dreams, or going round the city putting up mad broadsheets. THEY would always win the information war. Soundtrack: traffic, splashing behind a small paneless window cut in the kitchen wall to ventilate the tub, and one day a SHOT, when a man sticks an automatic out the garret window opposite and kills another walking down the sidewalk.

    Left for the left …

But what impetus, exactly, gave 'story' the rush of something new: these written ghosts of subjects, fragile substantives, compiled from public text, experience, and facing the world obliquely? Memory can't resist proffering, in answer, one last dream for analysis: the [above] *Dream About Writing*. Which, thus prodigiously deconstructed, yields a trace of abjection [*lying, sloppily, in bed*], a whiff of betrayal [*three + oblique*]. Precisely those elements that trope the vaguely comic autobiographical conjunction of semiotics, semantics, gossip, what she now thinks of as prose; 'experimental' inasmuch as implying failure to represent the universal, linked to class, gender, sometimes race, but also to the pleasure of sounding out, a kin to poetry. Sometimes she watches, regretfully, as her little tales float, textured, suggestive, by the averted eyes of certain poets she admires. Who, along with lovers of more conventional fiction, persist in reading 'experimental' prose for content or 'voice' alone. As if a subject redistributed across hazardous abutments, torqued by inner syntax in dissonance with outer, or the reverse, can be absorbed as passively as a drugstore novel. Our group would have laughed even *then* at the poster a young poet, two blocks up, has on the wall of his borrowed room. Citing a famous novelist saying every sentence has a truth waiting at the end. Manifest truth maybe, we'd have mouthed, red lips insulting.

↪ i.e. latent?

Recently [plus ça change]:

Some French-language ESL students, reading these stories, smile at what they call 'the repression.' In bed with her bathing suit on??? They also smile at those incontinent raspberries blooming on the snow [another dream, I'm afraid]. Was she New Age? Influenced by the cinema? The mid-career writer, on her platform, tries to explain how Wild Strawberries, seen at seventeen in a repertory cinema, made her feel so free she floated out, past trashcans, toward a future of broken narratives. Why? they smile again. Because we wanted difference, we wanted everything. Here the twenty-year-old heads from Ville Brossard,

Ha!

Time.

Kenya, Hong Kong, Stockholm and Chicoutimi nod. And because we wanted everything, adds the writer quickly, we totaled Marxism + surrealism + new theories about the death of the western subject into the equation. While a plethora of identity issues screamed in the background. On streets called Rachel, Marie-Anne, Jeanne-Mance, cafés were full of feminists discussing language, and the eruption of the anteriority of language within it, the latter identified with Mother [Kristeva]. We wanted to circumvent *logos*. Without somehow abandoning a towering lucidity. Some of us were also seeking to locate, semiotically, the unique sounds of a French-dominant multi-linguistic city.

Dear R: Walking in Prospect Park, green light glinting off shiny grassblades, the gleaming hole in the distant Manhattan skyline, which only the familiar – I guess I mean any global citizen with access to a screen – recognize as absence: you ask the same questions I often ask myself. Re: relationship to reader. Re: the alleged superiority of poetry for allowing singularity of perception, bringing focus to bear directly on words and the sounds of them. And relations between. I love the hugeness of your desire for reaching the highest point of expressivity in art and life [Maiakovsky]. Do not certain conjunctures foster this kind of raw energy required for pure invention? Skating between modes and limitations. Less acknowledged: what I am learning from you …

Yet, albeit, at the same time, furthermore:

She wanted to touch Her with her statements. Notwithstanding the faint whiff of complicity with dominance connected with speaking assertively. Was 'to sentence' a border issue? Controlling?

Paranoid in its insistence on contiguity. Twas a journalist, cigarette on lip, bad liver, sensitive crinkled face, who'd told her: 'A sentence starting with *To tell the truth* is unreliable, discombobulated, corrected.' Was not any sentence such? She wanted to turn them into lines of flight, translating provisorily, and yes, naturally *belatedly*, the drift of experience. Hopefully her perpetual avant-garde urge to underscore, again and again, that contiguity between making art and life, would not grow rigid. [Here, she gets an image of paper handcuffs and – sex.] But we live in chaos. Is not a tendency to endlessly interpret, to graft 'sense' onto 'nonsense,' both attribual to paranoia – and sensible? It amuses her to think that Freud's case of female paranoia ['Essay Running Counter to the Psychoanalytic Theory of Paranoia'] momentarily derailed his whole paranoic system. Implying, as it did, that his female client's fear of being poisoned appeared to originate less in Mother than in her social context. But ... can a bride in a wedding NOT embrace the family? Only *later*. Still she wants to write prose. Why should only Poetry [be] ... about the way language works (rhythms and sounds and syntax – musical rather than pictorial values) as much as it is about a given subject [Ann Lauterbach]. Me too, I wanted to create meanings at multiple sorts of intersections.

•

It's April again. On the radio they're saying a chunk of Antarctica, the size of PEI, is collapsing into icebergs. A CBC journalist chirps about the advantages of global warming – for gardeners. Much extended growing seasons. Of course the bugs will get a foothold. Bug oils advised. Feeling weird, I turn it off. If dread seems part of who we are, maybe to recount is to launch reasoned if defensive resistance. Camped up with lipstick. Like women during war.

Outside a pair of sparrows fornicate on a bough. Turn the radio on again. An astrologist beams to the story-teller in me that there's a bigger plan at work. Look forward with hope. Tanks roll into Hebron. France votes right; *then* marches left. You never know, bubbles the astrologer, what lies around the corner.

I veer off l'Esplanade, still in the dark, onto the walk that bifurcates the park. Toward the public washrooms. That old angel monument visible in the distance. A woman approaches, holding a black umbrella blindly before her. A homeless man with his cart full of plastic bags bikes by, holding high a bouquet of florist-wrapped flowers. Such instants, innocent almost, are where stories begin, breathing in and exhaling ... not the single breath of a single genius, Breton's mythic poet having been dumped, thanks to language feminists and others, for more collective and material notions of aleatory writing. Walking I am thinking how Mayan poetry was considered a parallel translation of what the Gods said: only some words grasped and interpreted, implying the rest. These stories, though not on the whole set in Montréal, could not have been written without being ensconced at the time of writing in the intense, effervescent political and writerly debates taking place in late seventies and eighties here. Evolving, over time, into a random method of collecting public and private text, including electronic, that I am still trying to coax into prose.

And that brings us again to the impetus that determines choices. I address this last to those who call *Spare Parts* 'Gail's book of poetry.' Also, to Michael, George and others who began writing wonderful experimental prose, so inspiring, then shifted to participation in the construction of the last twenty years of Canada's strong canon. I find it odd that a critical field of radical poetics has grown out of that era, but little in the way of an interpretative milieu for experimental prose – by which I mean prose that redistributes notions of subjectivity, time, through investive layering of narrative and language. The lack of encouragement of prose that can also be read denotatively [i.e., is layered, allusive, metonymical] has resulted in a remarkable reduction of reading possibilities in Canada. Such work suffers from lack of critical attention to the way language, thought, operate, in favour of its often torqued narrative. Recently, the Globe and Mail went so far as to say such writing does not exist. No visible writing about Montréal in English has existed since Leonard Cohen and Irving Layton, until the present. In a country where so much of life takes place on the cusp of difference, you'd think the space would exist, even be welcomed, for the kind of intra-genus performance that takes place when alterity meets. *(otherness)*

These are the young stories of a writer already suspicious of looking back. The fact that my early attempts [notably 'Tall Cowboys,' 'Withdrawal' and 'Petty Thievery'] lean on dreams and solitary automatic writing, on characters who seem more like figurations, a little campy, is linked to an already impossible-to-avoid sense that 'telling' itself is not transparent. 'Telling' could only be telescoped from some fragile angle, an angle itself obviously wanting – motivated by a faint paranoia linked to the porosity of the subject. Contrarily, inner and outer syntax contained sufficient identity issues to render irresistible the playing off of formal investigation against the junk food of nostalgia, notably its media version, popular culture. I remain a writer who feels at her best in intense dialogue with the present, who thinks of a writing subject as being elided by material conditions and awareness, pressed on by time, flight, context – an approach I suppose some might call 'rhizomatic.' Which, in 1981, when these stories were published, was in the air as a concept, albeit conjuring, predominantly, buttons of gathered roots under the brown surfaces of lily ponds in stagnant back waters of the polluted Castor River flowing through the opening pastoral 'Climbing the Coiled Oak.' Its protagonist's faux-rural innocence [with her bottle of Magic Lite] embarrasses me a little [I was an airforce brat]. From 'Ottawa' on I was better able to apply the constraint of mocking the sound of print journalism that became the intent of this project. Each subsequent book-length narrative work has been framed by some formal limitation, though not applied rigidly, aimed at avoiding what I loathe most in writing: sentimentality. I only hope that the substantial audience currently emerging for experimental poetry will open a door to the possibility of more denotative reading of non-transparent narrative. A sentence, after all, is a device, like any other.

CLIMBING
THE COILED OAK

*S*pring came through the gully bursting wide the creek edges where I lost my grandfather's watch. That was the time I found Rita McQueen and a boy in the pine thicket where we used to play hide-and-seek. Rita's jeans were down at her knees and her bum was covered with needles. I was eight. My heart beat quickly. Rita looked surprised for a moment. Then she laughed and pulled the boy down on top of her. She didn't care. Rita McQueen didn't care about anything.

Rita McQueen washes in mud
Rita McQueen has a big ⦻⦻⦻⦻
Rita McQueen Rita McQueen

Rita McQueen swept through her door and closed it quickly. A snowball bounced off the window. 'Boys will be boys,' my mother said. In this case she was not referring to their treatment of Rita

McQueen. She looked at me worried. I walked by Jimmy Miller's clubhouse. I took off my coat even though there was still snow on the ground. Mother was watching through the window behind the oak branches. You could see the new-sprouted tits on the front of my T-shirt. Jimmy spotted them even from where he was standing at the end of the laneway by the clubhouse in his Uncle Achilles McMaster's toolshed.

I walked back. I could hear them laughing inside. 'Hey, com-ere, we've got something to show you,' he said. I looked like I didn't want to but could be persuaded. 'Hurry up,' said Jimmy.

I went in, walking quickly but not running. The guys were sitting around with rakes and shovels looking pretty tough. We girls had a clubhouse down by the river except for Rosy Deguire whose father beat her with a hockey stick and we wouldn't allow in. The boys never paid us the compliment of a visit.

'Ya ever hear the song Davy Crockett?' asked Denny Armitage, spitting on the floor.

'Sure,' I said, a little fazed by the air of conspiracy, and started to sing:

> 'Born on a table top in Tennessee
> Killed him a b'ar when he was only three.'

'Stupid girls, I knew she'd say that,' said Denny. They sang, keeping their eyes on my T-shirt:

> 'Born on a table top in Tennessee
> Killed his mother when he was only three
> Drank a case of Labatt's 50
> Davy, Davy Crockett.'

Outside Rita was going by grinning with her little brown boy. I hurried over to my house standing behind the big branches of the coiled oak. 'Was that Rita McQueen I saw you with just now in front of Achilles McMaster's?' asked my mother. 'I just saw her coming out of Arty Granger's garage,' she added to my father who was sitting at the table. Her lip twitched. 'And you stay out of that clubhouse, do you hear?'

I went into the living room and sat down on the blue-and-white checked sofa to wait for supper. Behind me was a hole in the wall put there by my brother's hockey puck. The hole had accidentally been included in a family portrait which my mother ordered at great cost. We sat around her all looking very thin in the shiny black-and-white print. The hole stood right over my head.

April Lily hid behind the telephone pole by the ravine. She was thirty-three and in Grade Three. Her sister Joy peed on the floor and soaked it up with her handkerchief. You could hear the little streams rushing down the ravine through the melting snow. There they joined a bigger stream which raced by Rita's cottage at the end of the ravine, under a culvert, and smashed into the Muskrat River. We were hiding in the pine thicket waiting for the school bell to ring. I watched Martin McCoon's juicy red lips and his teeth that stuck out so he always seemed to be smiling. 'Okay,' he said. 'They've all gone in.' We slid down the gullyside to the crick. Rita watched from her cottage where she lived with the Indian. Nobody knew his real name. He would stand by the general store across from Horner's Hotel and show us how his kid could smoke. He would let us pound the metal plate in his chest. He said Rita was really strong and scrubbed floors right up until the baby was born. He said it didn't hurt a bit.

My mother was furious when she heard that and told us not to talk to him.

Jimmy Miller had a bottle of beer from the teacher's cupboard. We lay down in the sun on the steep slope. The snow ran past us toward the crick, making us wet on the bottom and warm on top like rocks in a spring pond. I moved closer to Martin who was passing beer back and forth to Jimmy. His lips were so red they could have been bitten off an apple. I saw them open and close around the beer bottle. Martin noticed me looking and started to smash Jimmy.

After that we built a fire in the curling rink on Bottom Street to dry out.

That's how we got caught. April Lily saw the smoke and told somebody. We threw stones at her and went home.

My mother stood by my bed. She said I'd caused her eleven years of pain. In the field outside the window I could see the egg-shaped horse about to colt. With my brother's BB gun over my shoulder I set out for Lamb's Bush behind our house. From the outside it looked tight, with the tree arms all wrapped around each other as if you weren't allowed in. But as soon as you stepped through the branches and ferns it made you feel safe and you couldn't hear anything but the creek gurgling. My dog Randy broke the ice and went for a swim. I drank sap from the maple pails. We stayed all day. When we went back in the evening everything felt fine inside. But the village was a bit crooked. I thought I saw my mother in the neighbour's bed which was impossible. She never went near his house.

The teacher phoned and said he was coming over to explain why I wasn't permitted in school for a while. He said it was one thing for me to miss classes since my marks were fine and another thing for Jimmy and Martin who often failed. He sat on the blue-and-white sofa watching them send me to my room until I knew better. The branches outside my window were covered with ice. Then the

24

ice melted fast and the buds came. At dusk the birds flew round. I closed my curtains because I was afraid there might be vampire bats like in Dracula. The buds got fatter until they would burst and the village was as warm as red brick, except on Sundays when the houses seemed black and white and the grass by the river silver.

They let me out.

I ran down the street to the restaurant where we hung around after school, Martin, Jimmy, Carmel and me. Carmel had pierced ears and was one of The French, but never spoke it. She lived on the Bottom Street with April and the others, but she was smart. She pretended she hated boys and always got the first turn in the Bluebell, a dresser drawer Martin made into a boat.

My stomach felt like when you go away for a while and you don't have to care what everybody thinks and then when the car is coming over the bridge where it says McMasterville, Ont. Pop. 310 you start getting a nervous stomach.

Carmel took one look at my hair and said, 'Ugh.'

My mother didn't like it much either. I did it in my room. One coat of Magic Lite for each night I was there.

Rita McQueen went by on her horse toward the bar-hotel swinging door. Her milkweed silk eyes were sad. The Indian had disappeared. She said he'd gone up north to work in the mines and something terrible had surely happened to him.

Everybody else said you couldn't expect an Indian to stick by his wife, especially when she wasn't his wife. (Haw, haw, haw.)

I sat down anyway with Martin and Jimmy and Carmel. Across the road was a red-brick building with square letters carved in cement that said:

REGISTRY OFFICE

BIRTHS, MARRIAGES, DEATHS

It grew warmer. Rita hitched up her horse by the hotel near where the road dips down over the bridge. Rosy Deguire used to walk on its broken railing and threaten to fall in. Hardly anybody ever tried to stop her. Then Rita came and sat on the bench in front of the Registry Office. She took off her sweater and lit a cigarette. Martin, Carmel and Jimmy giggled. At last, just to spite them, I crossed the road and sat down with Rita. She looked at my gold hair and smiled a little. After a while she said to me: 'You know, I don't care what they say. I feel fine the way I am. I haven't even got any stretchmarks.' I looked at the reddish hairs on her brown arm. Her eyes were like a cat's when you pour it a saucer of milk. I looked at her arm again. Something inside, as far away as the grass under my feet, made me want to touch it. My music teacher passed, carrying a teapot. I couldn't concentrate. I looked away from the arm. Down the street on the steps of their falsefronted house the Proulx sisters, who were waitresses in the city, painted their fingernails bright red. I wondered what stretchmarks were and could think of nothing to say.

The wild strawberries popped up in the fields by the tracks. When the clock on the station turned to train-time you put your ear down to see if the train was coming. You also watched for the poison ivy springing from under the rails which afflicted the neighbour's wife so she couldn't have underwear. And for Harry the Hermit who pissed himself and killed someone with a knife, according to our Sunday School teacher who was the minister's wife.

But Rita was not afraid. She walked right over the tracks every day except on Sundays when she rode with her father while her mother and deformed sister put on their flowered hats to go and sing in the church. I would meet them on the way home from Sunday school, Rita's auburn curls bouncing and the auburn tail of the horse.

However one Sunday Rita was on their farm porch peeling potatoes, waiting for Evelyn and Mrs McQueen who hadn't come home from church yet. That was before it was out she would have a baby. On the trees you could see the sticky white tents full of thousands of brown caterpillars, except on the apple trees because they were covered by blossoms. I reached up my hand to pick some of the beautiful white flowers. Down on my head came a shower of worms. Rita's face laughed until the potatoes bounced on the floor. My mother's forehead wiggled into a frown.

'Evelyn is such a lovely girl,' she said on the way home. 'She's not beautiful but her inner sweetness shines forth. I hope you turn out like her.' She looked at me. My head was leaning back on the rough woollen seat of the old Plymouth. My feet didn't touch the floor yet. *inner /outer → strange, vague comment*

I sat in the sun on the bench in front of the Registry Office. It was getting almost too warm to sit there. You could see the footprints in the pavement of the roadside. Carmel and Rosy sauntered over and sat down beside me, sticky tight, as if I was made of tar. They started whispering things behind my back. My stomach felt empty and black. We got up and moved across the street. The heat came at us in waves. Flies flew around the faded Neilson's Ice Cream sign in Winton's window. We moved in a cluster into the restaurant. Harry the Hermit sat smelly at one end of the counter and Rita at the other. I managed to slide in next to her. Her cool arm coming out of her dress felt beautiful against mine. Gary Winton served us ice cream, watching our blouses with his white potato eyes. Behind him the sticky flypaper flew back and forth in the current of the fan. I imagined the reddish hairs of Rita's arm rubbing up against the darkish hairs of my own. Like cats. Cool and warm. Sugary-vinegary. 'C'mon upstairs. We got something to show you,' said

Carmel in a tough voice. She and Rosy were both good fighters, so I said 'See ya' to Rita and went up with them into an old warehouse full of tires. 'Ever smoke?' said Rosy, pulling a pack of Export A from the front of her blouse.

'Sure,' I lied.

We lit up. The heavy smoke kicked into the back of my throat.

'Inhale,' said Carmel. It was an order. I drew in and the feeling in my stomach turned from black to green. After that we climbed up on the parapet of the Orange Lodge and looked down on the village, thinking we were pretty smart. A cool wind came up.

The hot clouds gathered in the sky. My father drove down the road. The milk bottles were lined up on either side, dividing the village like at elections: the squares for Protestant-Conservatives, rounds for Catholic-Liberals. It was the beginning of the milk-bottle war.

My father stopped to pick us up. He said the whole thing was getting out of hand. Arny Chalmers, who sold his milk in the squares, was losing business to Armand Côté of the rounds. It was affecting Arny's ability to give to the Amalgamated Church of the Lord. 'Hop in,' said my father who in his capacity as treasurer felt the situation imposed a discussion.

We went over the hills and over the orchards and over the bridge where Arny Chalmers' bustiest daughter who was thrown out of Dorothy Blair's party for letting a boy feel her up was switching cows in the dust. We could see Mrs Chalmers' apple-dried face behind the screens drinking lemonade with some of her children. Arny was absent.

Solly and I sprang down to the river. It warbled cold and fast. Suddenly Solly yelped. A crab was caught on his foot. I killed it with a stick, hurting his toe. He cried. But then we saw Arny's truck standing a little downstream. We ran along the damp bank. I reached it first and looked over the hood. On the grass sat Rita dressed like a queen in a crown of millions of dandelion chains. Arny was crawling toward her on his knees, buttercup horns coming out of his brushcut and his thing sticking straight out of his pants. I dropped my stick and ran.

A wagon was rumbling along the Low Road. It stopped for some children. A little girl stood back in the dust, shaking her head. She wasn't allowed.

We climbed in the car. My face was red. My mother slowly shook her head as she listened to what Solly said. 'That poor woman,' she sighed. She didn't mean Rita of course. I stared out the back. The little girl dropped her lunch box and ran after the wagon. They pulled her on. It bumped down the road behind us.

We went home and sat on the verandah, waiting for the storm to come. The wind whipped the dust along the road and the mosquitoes left big red lumps on the back of my brother's neck.

Mrs Chalmers came to Cassie Carlyle's wedding dressed in black. Arny's place in the choir was empty. The minister preached a sermon about how a man oughtn't to take a wife the better to serve the Lord, but if he must he must. I imagined I was small enough to sit up high on the church rafters. It was so beautiful up there in the stained-glass sunbeams. The bride left the church on a wagon covered with Kleenex roses.

It was night. I walked through the milkweed fields as starry with white pods as the starry sky. There were clocks in all the village crotches. They sat on their verandahs, rocking and ticking. I slipped into the narrow path of the ravine that led to Rita's door. She had the biggest clock. It was ticking loudly. But her milkweed eyes were crying. All the windows in her house had been broken.

It happened after the Orange Parade. The Protestant boys followed it through town bashing all the bilingual signs. There was one on the corner of the ravine above Rita's that flashed STOP ARRÊT day and night. They threw rocks to erase the ARRÊT and some of them kept right on going through Rita's windows.

I opened an eye. A ball grazed by. Carmel was jumping up and down punching her catcher's mitt. 'Get it,' she screamed. The crickets were chirping sort of high-strung. The dry grass made us prickle and itch. I could smell the sweat and powder on the pimply face of Corrie Lynx. Her mother Rose was a lady of disrepute. Corrie lay beside me tracing faces from true confession cartoons. She always did that. We were the only girls not good enough for the ball team so we spent time together even though at home they told me after Rose and Corrie moved in next to April Lily who lived next to Jocelyn Judgement and her preaching parrot who lived next to Arty the Addict who lived next to Carmel's family of twelve kids: 'Harlots. Now I don't want you hanging around on the Bottom Street anymore, do you hear?'

When Carmel heard I wasn't allowed near her place she told everyone I let Martin feel me up the day we played hooky.

Homer Penney wrote Onomatopoeia on the board. He swung the pointer at it like a baseball bat. Our hands went up. Our dresses stuck to our bums. The wasps buzzed in the heat. Someone said: 'The way the wasp sounds when it hits the fan, sir, that's onomatopoeia.' Everyone laughed and he let go a volley of books. It became quiet. We started putting up our hands to leave the room: one finger for a drink at the fountain in the cloakroom, two to go to the toilet in the basement. From there it was easy to sneak off to the swimming hole. Just out the side door and right on down the road. I got there first. June was the best time for swimming.

The river was still going fast enough you couldn't smell it. Macky March, who had a fat black cat and a yard full of old car wrecks, was floating by on an inner tube singing Cruising Down The River. You could see part of his hairy black thing where his bathing suit was coming down.

Suddenly Martin was running over the hill. 'Quick,' he shouted. 'Into the shed. Penney's coming.' We ran up the ladder and squeezed behind some haybales in a corner. On my arm I could feel the breath coming out of Martin's red mouth in short fast spurts. 'He caught Dorothy Blair,' he said. 'She was coming down the stairs and I was halfway across the yard when I heard him scream at her.' We sat still, very close. A smile slid onto my face. Martin would hate me if he saw it. He would say to the others he was stuck there with me. Ugh. Footsteps came into the shed and started toward the ladder. Homer Penney was wheezing like a rusty chainsaw. We waited. The only thing that moved was Martin's hand. He grabbed my tit. He knew I wouldn't say anything with Penney standing there on the ladder. I looked at Martin's juicy mouth. Penney sounded like he was having a heart attack. I moved his hand just a little aside. He let it fall. Penney was breathing a little quieter. My breasts stood up round as oranges. My stomach hurt. He wasn't putting his hand back. Maybe I moved it too fast. Penney started backing down the ladder. Martin's apple-red mouth came close to my face. I could feel his breath on my cheek. 'Unbutton your blouse,' he said. The footsteps were going out of the shed.

'Oh no,' I said. This could really ruin my reputation.

'Well then I'm going.'

'Well maybe you can just see.'

He looked. 'Not very big.'

'How about you? Are you big?'

31

He showed me. It was pink and hard. My nipples stuck out as if they were staring at something. Between my legs it was as wet as the gully in spring.

'I heard you like it,' he said. Then he was on top of me. A Coke bottle rolled back and forth noisily under my back. I could feel his thing against my underpants. Each time my head came up over his shoulder I could see a big red and white sign on the opposite wall that said Coca-Cola. It was Mr Winton's shed. I wiggled harder, hoping to feel him against my bare skin. But it was too late. There was a rush of wet on my cotton crotch. Martin got up and left without saying a word. There was a funny look on his face.

'Your shoes are dirty up the back,' said Solly when I got home.

The sky turned hot-pink like the top of Alan McCoon's two-tone Chevy and then black. It was a little cooler than the day. After track practice we walked home through the milkwood fields. Martin walked with Carmel. The night came over the fields full of milkweed pods shaped like Rita's eyes and through the empty ravine and through Rita's empty house. Nobody knew where she was. We walked by the schoolhouse where the school board was having a meeting about the swimming hole incident.

'It's clear,' they were saying to Homer Penney, 'that you've not won their respect.'

'It's clear,' said my mother when I got home, 'that you have no respect. You should be in a convent.' I saw nuns flying down the white walls like Dracula.

I was sent to my room where I would stay every night after supper until I learned better. I knew it would cost me. Martin would blab if I wasn't around all the time to make sure he didn't. Outside the window I could hear the bats coming out of the trees by the balcony. They were like nuns. Carmel was like a nun.

They were all like nuns. They were whispering: 'She likes it, she likes it.'

I dreamed they got caught in my hair.   *bats*

Carmel's eyes dug into my back.

Jimmy Miller's pencil dug into my back.

Homer Penney's tobacco-stained fingers trembled as they picked up the chalk and wrote Radisson and Groseilliers on the board. We couldn't pronounce their names, except Carmel. We'd end up saying Groseilliers like Gooseberries and everyone would giggle, even Penney. Maybe he wasn't mad, after all. Dorothy Blair tried a snicker.

'Well,' cried Penney. 'You're so smart you can go swimming on school time. Let's hear you say these names.' She couldn't. She had red hair and a red face. He stepped closer. She tried again. He slapped her, swinging his arm back and forth until she was snow-white. She fell back into her chair.

After the bell rang we ran down to the frog pond in Lamb's Bush. Dorothy's face was black and blue. Little bells twinkled in the treetops. Bloated frogs swayed serenely on the lily pads in the brown pond. Dorothy picked up a board with a nail in the end and went splatt. A frog fell over and rolled belly-up in the pond.

99 frogs were having a ball

but one of the frogs just happened to fall

now 98 frogs are having a ball.

The frog floated away. Its orange flesh looked sticky under the torn green skin. Dorothy's fat freckled arms brought down the board again. Splatt. Ninety-eight frogs were having a ball ... Dorothy grunted out of her blue face. The orange frog-flesh made me feel like throwing up. Dorothy's fat arms flapped the board down again on the water, faster. Faster and faster the frogs began to flop off the lily pads and float away bleeding green and orange in the brown water. The birds began to get excited. They hopped from branch to branch. The little bells clanged brighter and brighter. I began to feel sick only as the nail sank into the skin. When it came out and the frog fell over a nice feeling floated up my legs. I leaned as far as I could over the frogpond. Splatt splatt flop flop. Dorothy groaned, the frogs garromped, the birds screamed, the trees rang. It was quite a racket. But finally the last frog flopped over and Dorothy and I fell down on the grass.

Then I noticed the pond was the colour of burning cinder dotted with floating green blobs. The sun was going down. I was late for supper again. I ran.

All of the Protestant village was heading for the Amalgamated Church lawn where the fresh white tablecloths were held in place by bowls of purple flowers. The grass was the greenest of green, the river was gurgling, the birds were singing and fruit blossoms were filling the air. It was the best time of the year. It was strawberry social time.

Solly and I started out across the field. I was wearing a beautiful meadowgreen flowered dress. The milkweed pods were ready to pop. We squeezed them with our hands and the milk ran through our fingers. My stomach was full of butterflies because I was afraid they were saying I was easy to feel up. I could see them sitting there on the bench in front of Winton's saying it every night I was made to stay in my room. People were coming down the curved road along the river from their red-brick houses and their white false-fronted houses. The farmers were coming over the potholed roads in their dusty cars. They smelled of soap and manure. I could see the back of Martin's head going through the blackberry patch behind the church. And down below, Rita McQueen, her lips painted red and smiling, was coming out of her house in the ravine with a stranger. They started down the road. She looked very happy wobbling on her high heels and in her low-cut dress. He was handsome. But I couldn't see them yet.

The church ladies held their fluffy creamy plates of shortcake high as they marched among the tables, skirts and violet-perfumed powder smells blowing in the breeze. I looked for Martin's red lips. I caught them at a table with Carmel, who wasn't supposed to come because she's Catholic. I decided to go over to them anyway. 'Hi,' I said. Carmel looked hostile so I added: 'What are you doing here anyhow?'

'She came with me,' said Martin authoritatively. He was fifteen. The butterflies began fluttering again under my meadow-green dress. Carmel waited until his attention was attracted by another tray of shortcakes, then she asked: 'You just getting back from the swimming-hole shed?'

I pretended I didn't hear, but my lip twitched. Carmel saw. My mother came out of the church basement with the coffee pot. I decided to help her. I wasn't supposed to be hanging around with Carmel anyway. Reverend McGillicuddy spread his flowing black sleeves, trying to get the congregation to utter grace before it was all gone. But the ladies were distracted by something else. Up the lawn came Arny and Mrs Chalmers in their first outing since the incident. Arny's face was red. They were given a place of honour. Then after a few more throat clearings and may-we-thank-the-lords, the minister was able to raise his wings over the people to pronounce the blessing.

'Good Lord … ' But some of the ladies were gasping, for up the lawn came Rita and her stranger. Her ankles wiggled in the straps that wiggled up the back of her shoes and her happy lips twittered as if she were nervous.

Reverend McGillicuddy turned on her, waving at her with his outspread wings like the Sunday morning a bat flew up from under the pulpit and he tried to scare it away. People began whispering and hissing. Somebody quoted from the Bible: 'Get thee away from me Satan.' Flustered hands knocked over plates of shortcake. Rita struggled to free herself from the batting folds of the minister's robe.

I sneaked behind the coiled oak on the church lawn, holding tightly to the tummy of my meadowgreen dress. Rita was my friend, but it wasn't for them to know. She crawled out of McGillicuddy's clutch, turned her back to the congregation and hid her face in her hands. I was shinnying up the trunk. The stranger looked at her, then clenched his fists, and punched the minister right in the chops. I reached the upper branches. The sunbeams shone through the leaves like they shone through the stained glass windows on the church rafters. It was nice. I decided to stay.

OTTAWA

The summery breeze blew the curtains. I lay in bed with my bathing suit on. Too hot. Then too cold. Now too hot. Very still. My knees drawn up in a hump. My mother taking her Sunday afternoon nap. The Sunday roast hardened in the oven.

That poor country boy was racing angrily toward the canal waving the portable radio he gave me hotly in his fist. (I couldn't help laughing. He bought one nobody made batteries for.) The pearl ring was in his pocket. I stretched my toes and cried a while. It was delicious. Then I noticed they'd stuck the plastic Mountie in the plant box.

The door slammed. The young Royal Canadian Mounted Policeman from the prairies came into the oak-panelled foyer. The organdy curtains fluttered. I ran upstairs. 'You'll have to excuse her,' said my mother to him, sort of embarrassed.

I sneaked out the back. My father was playing the violin. Turkey in the straw. He played it every Sunday. I'd sit on the verandah and listen. He wouldn't teach me. 'You're tone deaf.' I guess he felt kinda silly only knowing the one song. That country boy went by in a cloud of dust, braking sideways.

My mother called me into the parlour. I could feel the Mountie's thin lips. 'I want to tell you how to avoid rape,' she said. He was half-concealed behind the curtains. 'Boys are horrid when they don't feel so hot about themselves. So turn the other cheek. Stoop to conquer. Wear a white sweater.'

A solid gold Cadillac drove up outside. I went to the window. My mother pursed her lips. She has the Mountie's mouth. My father's is soft and wrinkled like overripe fruit. The Mountie stepped out from behind the curtains. The Caddy slid off into the sunset. I couldn't see who was driving. My cheeks turned pink. 'You're too romantic,' whispered my mother.

So when the bus passed I stepped on without a word to anyone. Soon we were driving by the canal. The moon made it blood red. It reminded me of the movie Moon River. We were entering the city of Ottawa.

MOON RIVER

Holly Golightly is the heroine. She is a gentleman's escort who manages never to come across. (No tits.) 'Change for the powder room please?' she asks. (She's quite classy.) They give her a fifty. She flees down the fire escape with it in the pocket of her skinny black shift.

The Y had two blue signs, one on each side of the road. YM and YW. Behind them the Peace Tower rose into the sunset. The third-floor room was hot and dusty. Yet if you opened the window a crack in came a strange chill. Down below the boys were stopping

40

at stoplights. They would take their hands off the wheels and put them under the girl's skirts (thinking nobody could see).

Francine in the next bed flicked on the radio. Elvis. I had my knees up. He has a way of saying words. Soft baby lips. Those fat cheeks of southern boys. They laugh quietly when they're in a mood to kill. 'You should see Chris,' said Francine. 'Ottawa's Elvis.' She was wearing a gold lamé bathing suit. Waiting for her underwear to dry. /gold.

YOU'RE WIDER THAN A MILE

We crept past Ramsay the receptionist. Me, Francine and the girl with the bandaged wrists. (Just a little razor-blade trick.) The moon was full. Chris slithered into the lights. Francine shoved toward the stage. He didn't give her a glance. I climbed into his gold Caddy.

His hand crept under my sweater. I was wearing a high-wire beauty bra. My nostrils quivered. Between my half-closed eyes I could see the moon bathing the road. A couple was kind of locked together on the front lawn. French-kissing. Chris brought his full lips close to mine, forcing my mouth open. I smiled, sort of embarrassed. He moved away. 'What I wanted was a natural woman,' he said.

They're tearing down Main Street for a shopping mall. Chasing the rats into the Rideau. I watched from the Y window. His picture's on top of Sally's Yukon Saloon. Between two high-rises. Francine smiled in her gold lamé bathing suit. (It gave her stretch marks.) 'There's a trick to French kissing,' she said. I could see her purple tongue in her deep throat. The Peace Tower rose palely at the end of the street. On the hill you could see the officers come and go.

41

Aunt Heloise was presiding over the roast. Her husband the officer smiled as my mother took a bite. Her lip twitched it was so juicy (compared to hers). My cousin Heloise invited me upstairs. Her big breasts bounced thoughtfully. She opened her dresser drawer. Inside, neatly stacked, were used Kotex napkins. Red-brown. She asked me if I wanted to share an apartment with her.

The moon shone ever brighter on the canal. Rideau Street was full of boys with chains hanging from their belts. And ladies in powder blue suits. My spike heel caught in the grille of the Capitol Cinema. The movie was Moon River. I went in again. Holly Golightly is running up the fire escapes. Chasing her cat. In her simple black shift. She runs smack into the arms of a writer. He keeps her warm. Beside me sat a short fat girl. Connie-the-concert pianist. She said she had the record.

Connie and I took her stairs two at a time. Her Moon River record was caught in a scratch. She disappeared through the chintz curtains. I could hear funny sounds coming from the roof. I looked out the window. When she came back in I said: 'Do you think Holly was a call-girl?' She laughed in her high sing-song voice. 'No she's an artist. And doesn't look back.' Lot's wife

I wasn't ready for the black-slip business. Ramsay was climbing the YW stairs. (I'd been watching the sunset.) She handed me my suitcase. Something about an underdressed woman in the window. 'Worse than Amsterdam,' complained the YM man (calling from across the street). Francine looked smug. I crept by that poor country boy playing his portable in the lobby. A gold Caddy passed. My cheeks were crimson. Connie said to meet her on The Driveway.

We slid down the rock terrasse. Elliott stood there, his thin legs among the drooping daffodils. His neck was surrounded with a Swiss collar. He looked hostile. On the other side of the canal, the

→ Prufrock

Russian ambassador cast a huge shadow on the stone wall. Elliott's father was caught in a Cold War scandal.

On the hill you could see the officers come and go. Speaking of Michelangelo (according to Aunt Heloise). The *Citizen* said the Chinese were going to overrun Canada. The geography teacher drew up a map. They needed the space. I was wearing a black shift, slim at the calves. Sick and tired of Teachers' College. My cigarette holder was concealed in my purse. The bus for the country came up outside.

My mother sat in the orange hall, waiting for the roast. Watching me with her dark eyes. Burnt holes in paper. My cousin Heloise was there too, dressed in smooth blue. 'Baked Alaska,' whispered my father, his weak mouth against my ear. 'Warm on the outside, cool as a cucumber in.'

The bus braked in the dust.

I climbed off at Connie's (close to the canal). I took off my clothes and crawled under the covers. Elliott came up unexpectedly. I threw off the blankets (the better to show off my Jantzen's 'slimline' bathing suit). He just stood there looking kind of worried. His legs were pretty skinny. Connie saw him the first time she crawled out on top of her roof. His family was moving in across the street. He said he'd brought me a book. He leafed through the pages for a few minutes and then left. He hadn't stayed long. I had the feeling he was saying to himself on the way downstairs: 'No class.'

I'M CROSSING YOU IN STYLE SOMEDAY

Aunt Heloise smashed a pimple and covered it with powder. 'We should strike at the Russians first,' said my uncle. Then she hid it in the shade of her organdy chapeau. Her skin smelled like fresh cream. There was going to be a garden party. The whole family set out for Parliament Hill. The pavement was hot and sticky.

'This isn't the swan song it sounds,' she murmured to me. 'I'm referring to a girl sitting in a beautiful cottage by a shiny river plunging down to a paper mill. She is playing solitaire and singing to herself. A man walks by. Hearing the voice he stops and stares through the glassed-in porch. "This is the girl I am going to marry," he says to himself. And he does. So you see, if it happened to me it can happen to you,' finished my aunt. 'Maybe,' I said, 'but I don't know how to sing.'

We kept walking. Chris's hit song wafted through a car window. Hands on sticky nylon stockings. 'Hasn't he called you yet?' said my mother. Taking me from behind. Yes we have no bananas. The new shopping centre smells of plastic. No he hasn't called. Yes the Mountie has moved to Manitoba. No the country boy … as far as I know he's still jerking his radio down the road. Like a drop stitched. I smiled. I don't look back. Another rock star rose out of the shingles over Sally's Yukon Saloon. Squeezed between two high-rises.

On the hill we could see the officers come and go. Drinking Pimm's. 'And avoiding husband-hunters,' said Aunt Heloise. People were spread in the prickly heat on the Parliament grass. The band broke into the Pirates of Penzance. Someone was washing a frog off the Parliament façade.

Heloise straightened her back. Diefenbaker went by in a buggy. A handsome officer was approaching. Mindful of Aunt Heloise's hint about husband-hunters I decided to be discreet. Only a small smile for my mother. But now the band was in a slow march. He moved on up the hill. Almost in time to the music. I looked at Heloise. Her sky-blue eyes were trained on another pair identical to her own. Buttoned tight in a tunic, to his chin.

I drew my knees close to my chest. My father used to try and force them down. (It was a game.) The ladies were dispersed on the grass in their Easter bonnets. Suddenly I caught sight of Connie lying on a car roof. Outside the grilled gate. I decided to take a stroll. A white potato face stuck out of the car window. 'I'm Gerry-the-General's-son,' it said, grinning. He handed me a mickey. I took a swig. There was a flutter of organdy beside me. My old Sunday School teacher grasped me in a tight embrace. The bottle was behind my back. She smelled of lavender powder. Underneath the pink roses on her dress I could feel her steel corset.

We drove slowly down The Driveway. Connie was stretched out nonchalantly on the roof in her black shift. 'You have bedroom eyes,' he said. Looking straight ahead. (They're brown. Like my mother's.) His mickey was between my feet. We came to the canal. The moon began to shine. Elvis's head came up behind a sand-dune. The neon lights were flickering around the billboard. Elliott stood knee-deep in the drooping daffodils. His father was fired.

YOU DREAM MAKER YOU

The job ad said: *Wanted: Cultivated salesgirl. Thirty yrs. or over. Well-spoken. French and English.* With the right makeup I could pass. I could wear a high-necked sweater and horn-rimmed glasses like Holly Golightly. When she was after the Iranian student prince. She would sit in the public library and study oil prices. He couldn't help but notice.

I walked by St. Griffith's-sur-le-Rideau. They were discussing Michelangelo and the Archangel. Whether theirs was an authentic copy of his. Or something. The saloon door beside the Church suddenly opened. Chris came out. You should see the tawny hairs on his golden chest. He wore a motorcycle belt buckle. His picture was surrounded by star-shaped bulbs. He watched my beehive hair-do passing in profile. 'You're too self-conscious,' he said.

The choir revved up into resurrection music. It was so hot the flowers on the Easter bonnets seemed to fade. Heloise's engaged! Aunt Heloise screamed with delight. Heloise had hot cheeks (for once). I shivered beside her ice-blue dress. My mother watched me sadly. One thing was for sure. I was leaving Teachers' College.

After the hot came the cold. The fog fell. The Peace Tower stuck up like a Sherlock Holmes mystery. Trying to see was like trying to draw tiny drops back from across your eyes. Veils of tears. A bicycle slipped through the daffodils. Elliott in a Swiss collar. In his hand a note for the Russian ambassador. 'Meet me by the match-mill,' he whispered. 'We can climb to the Chateau. The PCs are having a party.'

It's the party that gives the best parties. Gerry-the-General's-son was there. He gave me his mickey. I dropped it on the marble. We switched to a bottle of burgundy. Somebody complimented me on my spotless black sheath. 'Simplicity itself,' he said, grabbing my bottom. I complimented him on the spotless marble of his scalp, where his hair used to be. Elliott gave me some Russian schnapps. The red tunics twirled around. (Or was it me?)

Dief the chief was supposed to show up. They started rolling down the red carpet. In the corner of my eye I thought I saw Connie sitting outside the window. A smile on her lips. Someone said he was coming in a solid-gold Cadillac. A mollifier from the Americans. I stepped gingerly on the plush and started forward. Hoping to get a glimpse. Suddenly a chinless organizer was standing in front of me: 'Heh, heh, we'll have none of that here.'

I woke up in the fur coat room with a rug over my back. Waiting for cats. That was my first thought: waiting for cats.

Holly Golightly didn't wait for cats. She ran after them. That's how she found the writer. Chasing one up the fire escape. She felt cold. He put his arms around her.

My white hand stuck out the window. It was in the left wing of the Chateau Laurier. Down below the swans were skirting the whirlpool below the matchmill. I crossed the corridor and entered the elevator. 'Madame or Mademoiselle?' asked the elevator operator. It was dripping on the daffodils. The soldiers went by. I thought of sketching the Peace Tower. In the morning mist, two lips … It was a Craven A advertisement. Except it started coming closer. The soft red mouth.

Chris took my arm and we went back to the furry chamber at the Chateau Laurier. 'La Chambre Chatouillante,' he said. 'Madame or Mademoiselle?' said the elevator operator. Chris kissed me all over. The rock scene wasn't so hot. Elvis was turning Hawaiian. He started undressing me, kinda depressed. I could feel his velvet tongue. He took off my high-wire beauty bra. He said it was too bad I had such small breasts. 'Get dressed and I'll take you home.'

YOU HEART BREAKER

The record was still playing, so scratchy you could hardly hear the words. Connie was nowhere to be seen. I looked out the window. Across the way they were sweeping the floor of the new Hungarian Café. A girl came in with a mandolin under her flowing breasts. I don't know why but it made me want to have books.

That's when Elliott came up again. I was lying in bed thinking I'd build myself a library wall when he entered. He had a book in his hand. He kept leafing through the pages, looking at me like I wasn't listening. I was but I couldn't hear. A terrible racket had started up outside.

Downstairs my father's friends the non-commissioned officers were sitting in the back seat, singing 'Oh here we come all full of rum.' After Heloise's husband-to-be's stag. I got in the car. A chill swept in under the door. My father smacked his lips and said something. Baked Alaska? They all laughed, their mouths wide-opened. I got out.

A horn honked behind. Heloise's husband. Almost. I was still at Teachers' College, wasn't I? It would be nice if I could come to the cadet cotillion. Connie sat on the roof outside the chintz curtains. Perfectly silent.

WHEREVER YOU'RE GOING

My mother dreamed I was famous. Gail Groulx saves four out of six from flames, said the *Citizen*. Mme G. Groulx was struggling through the smoke with three of her children in her arms after her frying pan caught on fire when she suddenly remembered little Liette was left in her cot. Putting the three down she fought her way back for the fourth. Finally she staggered from the house, carrying all four. A huge crowd had gathered. The people cheered loudly.

Ottawa, 1962. The department store had no opening. I couldn't go back to Teachers' College. They said I'd spoiled my chances. I pulled on my tight white sweater and went to Parliament Hill to sketch the Peace Tower. Nobody noticed except a kid from the cleaning staff. He had a girl's name. Jocelyn. French. He wanted to go to law school but his father refused. 'Learn English first.' I looked at my paper. Maybe there was more to being an artist.

I'M GOING YOUR WAY

I chose wedding white. My mother said I could always come back to the country. A job at the egg-grading station. The breeze lifted the organdy curtains. My chest broke out in a red rash above the cardboard stays. My mother's eyes watched me dress. Connie was practising the piano. The notes were so high they hurt the eardrum.

The rain tinkled down. The silver limousine pulled away from Aunt Heloise's. My fake rabbit shortie was wet enough to smell a little like Campbell's vegetable soup. Heloise's husband kept his aristocratic nose straight ahead. The ballroom was awash with bright lights and tightly buttoned tunics. It was the national flag contest.

A quick shadow passed by the opened French windows, Connie, causing a small smile to tickle the corners of my mouth. At the same moment a pain began creeping unmistakably up the centre of my stomach. The band started. Oh you'll take the high road and I'll take the low road. Two cadets came crashing forward. I took the most sober. Jacques was laced up so tight in his tunic his neck hung over the edges. 'Be ladylike,' I said to myself. I thought of Heloise's well-kept hands. Was that something moist seeping onto my panties? Connie was in the window, her hand over her mouth.

The band broke into a souped-up version of the Pirates of Penzance. The damp air came in through the curtains. People marched around the floors by twos and by threes. (His friend had my other arm.) The full moon rose. They were stringing up the new flags. Red-tunicked cadets bordered each side of my white brocade. My slip got damper. Heloise chatted animatedly. The red spot spread outward. I could see her working her way behind me trying to see. Connie was heaving with laughter. Only moments before discovery. Chances are I wore a silly grin.

WITHDRAWAL

Around the house on Cherry Hill are raspberry bushes whose country-coiled berries grow on the very tips of stiff branches. Snow is no deterrent to the thriving of this fruit. In fact it seems to be in winter that it is at its reddest and ripest, so ripe it is almost falling off the soft conical tips of the fat branches.

I live in the house behind the bushes, which is shiny. Or rather, I lived there until one day I was sitting on my bed in my room, which is darkly panelled with pine-stained slats, looking into a cameo-shaped mirror. Suddenly, holding my chin in a certain way, my face became that of my mother. She died some time ago of a dreadful parasitical disease. There was no doubt about it. It was my face, and yet, seen from below while I held my chin pressed down sideways against my throat, it was exactly the face of my mother.

Soon after, I was speeding down the highway. It was a bright sunny day. The snow was well-ploughed. I raced along with the exquisite child in the back. My mother always thought this child belonged to her. Suddenly we were skating light as the wind back and forth across the pavement, the steering a loose too-pliable object in my hands. I awaited the sickening crash of metal, the split second when the oncoming stream of cars would be unable to concede. Make way for my dizzying spectacle! I awaited death as the sliding descending car brought the snow straight into my eyes.

A second of shock. I blinked. The child sat like a deserted rag doll on the white ground, limp, the skirts of her coat ecarted over her red and white striped stockings. But there was no blood. I knew immediately it was my mother had saved us. The thick line of traffic that ought to have been crushing down on the rigorous logic of my spiralling car was nowhere to be seen. The highway was bare.

CRESCENDO

I awoke on my bed in the dark-slatted room pinching myself to see if I was a ghost. She'd come back. I didn't know why. Unless I needed her. Maybe she needed me. Shadows fell across my face like the sun shining through a fence. 'I'll sleep with her if I want and her if I want. When I want if I want when I want,' he shouted. Inside me the house exploded. I wore a broken nose. Water leaked through the wallpaper roof of the sunken foyer. I could see all his teeth. (A priest in a white mantle led his flock over the mountain.)

Outside the raspberry bushes creaked heavily with their weight of fat fruit and frost. He slept deeply. A strange violin played over the snow. She did not appear before me in any sort of form. Nor could I hear her voice. But I awoke in the night and I knew she was there. Like a magnet she drew the words from me.

'You always said I won't get a man I don't know how to love,' I whispered to her. The violin struck a high note. The country-coiled fruit shivered. I showed her my eye which had turned black and blue, the blood vessels bursting on the side of my face.

'Maybe now you see things differently, eh? Look at you. You're nothing,' I said. The strange violin stopped moaning. The moonlight glittered off my teeth as I talked. 'Father's forgot. Married after the first winter. You gave him your life. Now look. No flowers on your grave.' I raised the cameo mirror holding it sideways under my chin. She stared down at me.

The wind and snow crackled around the shiny house. The exquisite child whimpered. He tossed and turned, chanting in tired tones, 'I love youu, I lovve yoou, yees Mary I love you,' then smashing the pillow and screaming, 'Stop asking stupid questions just leave me alone.'

The priest in the white mantle withdrew over the mountain. And with him my mother who'd become a Protestant during her life. On the other side was the glass restaurant where we once sat. The sky was the colour of honey. 'I love you,' he said. On the snow was a bouquet of roses. He put his arms around me. I climbed into his young chest occupying the place of his heart.

The doorbell rang until the house shook. The cross at the end of the road cast its shadow over the snow. 'Where's my baby?' I could hear her crying as he opened to her. She flew up the stairs, her body lightened by the parasite that consumed her, and knelt at the cradle by my bed. 'That child is divine,' she declared. The father stood by the bed taking the small pink fist in his hand. A slow smile spread over his soft rosy lips.

The house sparkled like a magnet in the sun. The raspberries were swollen and ripe. I lay on my bed in the dark room. She took over the child, dressing it in striped stockings and calico, playfully arranging its orange hair around its porcelain pink cheeks.

His beautiful body cast a restless shadow over the sheets. 'I know you two have been living in sin,' she said to me from behind the plump doll which grew wordless and bouncing on her knee. Her face was dark and wizened like an aging bird, and her lip twitched. He slammed the door.

'Besides, you never knew how to love,' she said.

The door slammed and he stepped into the light. I opened the door. The child sat on a shelf. In her hair the black-eyed Susans called black-eyed Saxons after her family name. I closed the door. I fumbled with my skis in the snow. Already he was far ahead and flying like a beautiful white bird. My body flailed heavily forward. I lunged after the rhythm of his beautiful muscle-bound body. Faster. He flew over an embankment and onto a flatboat floating down the river. At the other side stood a woman in flowing brown hair and thick glasses. I failed to reach the edge in time. The woman smiled. She reached out her hand. He stepped off the boat and crushed her in his arms. Her glasses fell to the ground.

''Twas my friends told me you two were living in sin,' said the dark birdface rocking in its chair. The dark cabinet with flowered wall-paper. The small hard smelly fæces fell into the china pot. The china doll smiled.

'And don't try and tell me it was platonic with that boy you went to California with either.'

The clock ticked urgently over the dark mantel. The raspberries bloomed like roses on the snow. I waited. She had her hand in the chocolate. 'You never knew how to love.' Some cherry fondue showed on her lip. I waited. He came into the warm. He shook off the snow. He took off his scarf and sweater. He tore off his tie and collar. 'This place is suffocating,' he said. I waited. The whisky tinkled tensely in the glasses. My stomach. 'You know,' he said. 'The road's so icy. I'm always afraid I'll get killed coming here.' I looked out the window. The reflection on the snow. 'Don't you see the roses?' I joked. It was an old joke. He didn't laugh.

The child whimpered. He paced up and down. I gave him another glass. He seemed better. I moved my queen. 'I love you,' I whispered, watching carefully. His knight moved out mute before him. I spoke the forbidden 'Where were you last night?'

'I need space,' he screamed. I could see all his teeth. 'My life is my life. Everybody does what they want. Understand?'

He left, slamming the door until the cut glass pane broke. I covered it with plastic so you could hardly tell. I put the exquisite child, fists clenched, into bed. On the dresser the face stared up at me from the cameo mirror. Outside the raspberry bushes creaked heavier and heavier with their beautiful fat fruit. I closed my eyes against the cool counterpane. A bat whispered against the window. The dark wings fluttered on the sill. She had come back. I could feel her in the dark.

'I can see you see things differently now,' I said. 'No flowers on your grave. You always said a woman mustn't be too romantic but a woman must know how to love. Hah.' Again I showed her the blood vessels bursting around my face.

On the road the little car careened from side to side, bouncing angrily off the snowbanks. His beautiful soft ripe lips were twisted bitterly. Suddenly he braked and smiled. A faceless woman with wavy black hair stood by the side of the road.

'Daddy,' called the child, though she knew we were alone in the house.

The priest in the white mantle led the flock over the mountain.

'You're living in sin,' said the bird rocking in the chair at the end of my bed. 'What did I do to deserve a daughter like you?'

We stood by the fire. The ice tinkled in the glasses. I tried to decipher his frown. His lips hung in dismay. Berry red. He turned them full face. 'You give me bad dreams,' he whispered. 'I dreamed you dissected my spleen. The living-in woman saw you do it and saved me. I could hardly continue my elections.'

I put my hand on his arm. 'I love you,' I said watching warily from the side of my eye. The wind sang like church music around the house. I saw the sun dance through the mosaic onto highly polished hardwood beams. My hand closed over the priest's, hot on the chalice. The rose slip showed under his white soutane. She marched me out of there into the Protestant church across the road.

'Time you learned some responsibility,' she said. My father stood stern in his black suit. She plunged her hand into the chocolate.

'Time you learned some respons– ' I suggested close to his soft lips. 'I want to live,' he screamed.

The wind cried in the attic. He was putting on his coat. 'No,' I whispered. My hand closed hot over his sleeve. He flung me crashing away from his chest into the stone wall by the fireplace. My nose.

'I love you,' I cried. The door was opened. He was fleeing, his silhouette sinking in the snow like Ozymandias in the sand.

COITUS INTERRUPTUS

The room was dark. In the attic the voice cried more persistently. I looked sideways at our semi-profile in the glass. Outside the raspberries waved ominously, deliciously in the night. I recognized the voice. It was my own.

She was close beside me. Perhaps even in my bed. 'I guess maybe I don't know how to love,' I said slowly. She lay there with her ragged gossamer wings. I could feel my nose swelling beaklike like hers.

The exquisite child stood in the door. 'Daddy,' she called, fearful. I smothered her in my arms. The limbs were limp. I caressed the porcelain cheeks. They were surprisingly soft. Slowly the little hands opened. The gossamer wings rustled restlessly at my side. We three. I dropped my soft package.

The stars danced in the sky like snowflakes. Far far away the violin. The gossamer wings. Suddenly dawn struck the window in pink stripes. I pushed the little limbs away from my waist.

He was driving down the road. His face hung to one side in repose as the caresses of the faceless woman worked up his body. On his breast pocket was a tiny bouquet of roses.

I went downstairs. Outside the old Seigneur's son stood staring at the house sparkling brilliantly on the snow in the first sun. The rang* reached below scarcely rippling under the small shadow of the cross. I found a cereal bowl and slipped into the light. I turned my back. He threw his body heavily over the horse and rode on up the road.

The raspberries were at their fullest and firmest, glistening on the snow. I hesitated. I took a soft tip in my cupped hand. The berry felt as if it would burst. In the field behind I saw a black shadow in the retreating flock make a swift flutter like a wing. I began pulling off the berries one by one. They dripped on the snow. I gathered the fruit in my bowl.

RETREAT INTO WOOD

Inside the house the limp-limbed child filled the room with her dark gaze. At the table also sat the shadow. Soon I would open the door. I'd tear the plastic off the cut glass. The sun would shine in in golden streaks. We'd be as radiant as raspberries. I'd be the host. And from the wooden bowl we'd drink a toast. Mother, daughter, bat-winged ghost.

TALL COWBOYS
AND TRUE

They left Annabelle, the last frontier town, tucked under an outcrop in the Rockies. She locked her sleeping children carefully in the house trailer. She took his hand. They walked along the Main Street. Horses and oil tankers, hitched to the same posts, fitfully pawed the sand, eyeing each other nervously.

They passed a poor cowboy sitting in front of a blind house. His faded knees jerked over the edge of the verandah. It was hot. He waited for the explosion of bullets that would never come. He feared taking refuge in the house. It was damp and dark. The cowboy preferred the risks of riding the trail.

They came to the edge of town. The man squeezed her close. 'Baby, you're beautiful,' he said. 'We'll go places.' The woman's hand hardened. He told her to stop worrying. 'Your sister will take care of your kids.' Back in the trailer camp the women played cards while they waited in silence from children's screams for the men to come in their loud boots, the beer gushing out of their bottles. She looked at his red sneakers and nodded.

They stuck out their thumbs in the dust by the side of the road. The cars went by oiled black. The metal waves reflected the sun painfully into her eyes. Behind her a crowd of ragged vultures cowered over a lying-down man. An old woman in sky-blue moccasins waded unevenly through the long grass toward him. After her ran a small girl with grasshopper legs. The young woman licked her dry lips and smiled at the child. Her man saw nothing. He lit a cigarette, his thoughts galloping confidently toward the sunset.

Her children were alone in the trailer. They slept soundly. It was hot. She wanted to sit. The pavement was sticky. She raised her head toward the horizon. It was blocked by the carefully ticking crotches of grain elevators. She looked wildly around. Behind her, out of a deep ditch, rose a powerful white charger. A cowboy stepped forth in rich embroidered boots and a cowlick. He motioned them into a bower of plush purple flowers. She took her place in the back between rows of blossoming shirts, her man in the front, and the great white beast retook to the ditch leaping forward between the cool day walls well below the burning gilt fields.

At last. She leaned back, breathing in the blotting paper perfume. Her man opened a soft volume of Lenin, his sneakers tucked noiselessly beneath him. The clay walls sped by outside. The children's cries receded. Through the rearview mirror the cowboy watched her. She ignored him and sighed. 'Twas a good ride. His eye fastened on her moist lips slowly smiling at how her father hated hitchhikers. Oh the children. The children alone. She quickly looked up. The eye was fixed on the button on her left breast. DES AILES AUX GRENOUILLES it said over a small blue frog with butterfly wings. 'You French?' asked a well-honed voice tightening like a lasso.

From behind the cool white columns of my verandah I watch Véronique Paquette walk by terriblement décolletée. The priest gives her shit every Sunday but she still does it just the same. Across the street Claude Bédard flirts on the front lawn with his girlfriend Bijou. 'Frogs,' says my father one of three bank managers all brothers. Drunkenly, they flex their flabby lip muscles at Véronique from their rocking chairs on the hot prairie. Then my father looks up at me and screams: 'Stick your nose back in that Bible. It's Sunday.'

'You French?' repeated the well-honed voice honed even higher.

'Non. No. Mais. Ispeakit.' A nervous tickle titillated the pit of her stomach. The cowboy's eye flinted like steel in the mirror. He shifted into pass and the charger rose above the deep ditch into dry fields flaring with the fluorescent yellow of rape. There could be a fire you know. What if the fields caught on fire? The children alone in the trailer. The eye stared steadily. Her man was unaware. He turned the pages of State and Revolution, his sneakers tucked snugly beneath him. She began talking to the eye quite fast. 'It's beautiful here. Blue sky up above. All you need is love … ' She stopped, guilty, ridiculous.

'Yeah.' The eye watched. The voice grew golden again. 'Big money on the gasline. Bad years back home I come up here to work.' The eye unlatched from her lips and pointed prayerfully toward the horizon still cluttered with wooden crotches. 'Seas of oil,' he said. The carhood shone in the midnight sun. 'You from near here?' she asked in a small voice. He took a picture from his breast pocket and passed it back. 'My mother and I farm in

Mackenzie.' The woman had a fair wide forehead like her son. Her lips were drawn back tight in a bun. On the back it was written: 'He who putteth his hand on the plough and looks back is in danger of internal damnation.'

INTERLUDE: A TRUE COWBOY IN LOVE

'Look Ma no hands.' The police car careens sideways across the road and hovers breathlessly over the high precipice. I put my hand on my stomach, staring at the perpendicular cliffs hanging below. 'Don't look back,' says the new hitchhiker (with red sneakers) to me and my children beside me. He winks in a friendly way. A clitoris pounds in a closet. My uncle has sold me a trailer to spare the family the shame. I am heading down the valley to hide my fatherless children. I will push it through the pass to Annabelle. The car tears away from the temptation and shoots into a curve. 'The thing about police cars,' says the fat young driver whose pants stink, 'is you can drive no hands to hold onto guns.' Close beside him on the front seat Ma smiles from under her greasy grey hair. 'I always buy police cars,' he says to us over his shoulder. 'The way we take off from stopsigns in Curstairs. Boy do the cops get peed off.'

Ma puts her hand close to his unsavoury crotch. He grins at her recklessly. We are descending rapidly as a white balloon toward the town where the trailer is. The cliffs become sandy like a setting from a cowboy movie sparsely henspecked with sage. But the cherry blossoms waft up from the valley below where the Ogo Pogo has just surfaced between the feet of a petrified waterskier. 'Maybe we'll see the Ogo Pogo,' says Ma. Her hand creeps closer to the crotch. He steps on the gas. We race through the town. There are cowboy boots on the hotel steps and frightened moustaches on coffee cups in the windows. On top of the false front façade it reads: CONFESS AND YE SHALL SAVE.

The charger cowboy's crotch was impeccable. His Adam's apple had tightened into a thoughtful knot. 'You know you French and folks in the east don't give prairie farmers their due profits for wheat flour.' At last her man looked up from Lenin. 'Capitalism,' he said. 'Centralized markets. You're too far from Toronto.'

The eye in the mirror turned momentarily toward him, but was intercepted en route by a six-inch fuchsia statue on the dashboard. It returned immediately to fix again on her face.

'Do you know the Lord?'

She looked out the window. The rape fields were still on fire under the horizontal rays of the midnight sun. It was hot in the trailer. The baby whimpered weakly while the three-year-old pushed the stool against the refrigerator door. She always did that to reach the handle and then of course she couldn't open the door because the stool was in the way. But suddenly the charger dipped again, not into a ditch but into a long narrow valley whose walls were cool blue green. The eye filled with a great grey light.

'This is called the Valley of the Peace,' said the voice. 'It was filled with fornicating good-for-nothings (excuse me miss he tipped his Stetson) with whom the settlers had to fight and teach how to farm.' They were approaching a long silver river. Aging deep-tanned faces rocked in rocking chairs in front of dilapidated wooden dwellings crushed by the ranch houses superimposed on their roofs.

'I don't feel so good,' she said to her companion. 'It's only a cat,' he said absently. His eyes were on the works of Lenin whose picture was strong and stern on the front cover. The fuchsia Christ smiled from the dashboard. The baby whimpered. She wished she could put a clothespin on his tongue. Peace. Now I'll have peace. Her father's hand is rummaging through the clothespin box. She feels the pain as he pries open her mouth.

The cowboy handed her a pamphlet. 'I am the way, the truth, and the life,' it said. She smiled sweetly, bravely, lips closed to hide her bleeding tongue. The tickle in her stomach turned into a giggle and rose to gag her. 'I've seen it before,' she said. Back in the trailer camp the boy was pushing a spoon between the baby's dried compressed lips.

'You mean you know Jesus?' asked the cowboy. His well-honed voice took on the timbre of a stained-glass window. 'It's always nice to meet someone else spreading the word of the Lord so that the peoples of the world can learn the errors of their ways.'

'That's racist,' she thought, spreading wide her legs in silent protest.

'That's racist,' said the Leninist, looking up from his book.

'Really,' she said, handing back the pamphlet. The hyenic laughter swelled within her. She squeezed her lips to keep it from hissing out. 'I've seen it … '

The cowboy stopped the car. He turned around to look at her. She snapped her knees together. 'You mean you know the Lord and you looked back. He who putteth his hand on the plough and looks back is in danger of internal damnation.'

The charger minced forward, uncertainly. 'I don't feel so good,' she said to her companion, putting her hand on her stomach. 'The children … ' He didn't seem to hear. He said nothing.

The brilliant quicksilver river approached. 'In his relationship with you,' said the voice, hued higher again, 'did Jesus uh hold up his end of the stick?'

'What d'ya mean?' she said. Like giant fæces the laughter moved into her mouth. The eye saw the fishtails glittering at the corners of her lips.

'Help,' she said to her companion. He didn't hear for he was furiously writing notes on the flyleaf of his book.

'The stick' said the cowboy more insistently, beginning to squirm in his seat. 'The stick. In his bargain with you did Jesus hold up his end of the stick?' Underneath like an error ran the quicksilver river.

The cowboy squirmed harder on his seat. 'The stick. Whose end of the stick?' he said louder. 'It was you who didn't hold up your end of the stick. It was, wasn't it? Wasn't it, huh? I know it was.'

INTERLUDE: A TRUE COWBOY IN LOVE
The police car is racing down into the valley, past the sagebrush into the beautiful cherryblossoms. 'It smells like cherry Chiclets,' says the son. 'I bet anything we see the Ogo Pogo,' says Ma. The hitchhikers have left. She fondles his pee-stained pants.

'I know Jesus,' cried the cowboy, rocking back and forth. He grabbed the statuette, waving it over his head like a lariat. 'Jesus never lets down his end of the stick. The stick … '

The car hit the valley wall with a thud. The red sneakers floated out the window, the laces trailing behind like spurs. The cowboy bled over the steering wheel, pierced by the statuette.

Her strawberry hair rose up the side of the valley. At last it was dark on the prairie. She sped through the cool night in her white shirt and white jeans. The baby was almost dead. She would get there before the headlines. In the first light of dawn she sped past the ticking-crotch silhouettes into Annabelle. The cops were coming toward her trailer with can openers. She sped through the dust past the poor cowboy's house. He slept on the rail, his spurs stuck in the wood. Gently (so as not to waken him) she untangled his legs and shoved his young strong body into the damp dangers of the forbidden house. She reached her trailer two strides before the police. Then she was fleeing, a child in each arm, their skin soft and warm against hers. New sensations were rising along her spine.

PETTY THIEVERY

We left Woolworth's. It was in a converted curling rink. A wagon wheel turned in the dust. In the April field a fist was clutched (from the last feminist demo). 'Hey Mom,' she cried. 'We didn't have to pay. I hid it in my hat.' 'Shh,' I said, looking around quickly. She dumped her booty on the snow. Bobbypins. Worth $1.33. Only $84.50 to go. We climbed into the car, careful to keep our feet up on the side so they wouldn't get wet from the hole in the floor. And headed toward town.

The crooked Castor overflowed in a browny line. Ice bursting its banks wider open'd all the time. Used to be as blue as the dust in heaven. I'd walk along it in my scarlet velvet suit. (Such a sweet smile, they'd say.) Now the frozen trees are crackling in the heat. And the city's moved down Highway 66. The river runs so thick. Heavy leather almost. Sinks in your stomach when you take a drink. Makes it hard to rise up in the morning. And once you're up, it's hard to go down.

Oh, Crooked shanks. Against the horizon. And a small red spot

The unemployment cheque had slipped out accidentally, into the stream. And floated off between the banks of ice. I guess I was concentrating on the car. Its motor was making such a melodic sound. Shimmering and shaking. When suddenly the rad spurted onto the ground. I leaned over the stream to get some water. Which wasn't easy. Because of the ice. I shivered. It grew dark. I looked up. The branches were covered with damaged birds. Then I saw the cheque was running down the river. 'Jesus,' I said. '$85.83. How'm I going to make up that money?' That's when I remembered the razorblade trick.

Out of the dust. The small red spot

The cheque sank in the grime. The kid and I boiled along leaving a white line. The motor idled faster and faster. The old Continuation School stood on the other side, its windows now all boarded up and vined. In front of it hung a hornets' nest. So natural. We used to sit there necking in the window seat while the hornets buzzed madly in the heat. Or fooling around. Wrestling but he got me with his football cleat. (Accidentally.) Right in the C. Keep smiling, otherwise you'll cry. It was then that the girl with the green eyes came up to me and said: 'Never mind, after school I'll show you the razorblade trick.' Her pink lips were laughing in my small ear, twinkling like minnows in a pond.

To change the subject I said to the kid: 'A steak would be nice,' pulling her over close beside me on the seat. I wanted to get some razorblades, too. We decided to go to Steinberg's. A wind blew up. The old trees were grinding like sheet metal.

The red spot, Vanishing. As in the drolerie of a vacuum

The motel sign stands on the corner. It's a fish in the wind. Beside it is a steak counter. They open it up in the spring. But a row of blue security men were standing in front of it. So all we managed to sneak was a can of Draino. Large economo size. I slipped it in her schoolbag. $2.79. Only $81.71 to go. Not that I need the stuff. You pee in it when you're pregnant. Keep a safe distance, though. You get brown for a girl. Green for a boy. (If any of the little particles fly up and penetrate flush with water for five minutes.) No wonder it never works. Should be B. for a B. and G. for a G. The meaning in metaphor. I know a woman who peed G. and got a B. who pared down his P. to get back to G. The fish on the wind-sign glistened like the girl with the green eyes.

Hotel closed, said the sign. The swelling red spot

'Come on closer,' I said to the kid. We drove by a girl sitting on a verandah. She was watching something coming out of the dust. When it looked like it wouldn't stop she stood up in her shorts and went out to wave it down. On the white line, Arms wide open'd. The driver smelled sticky sweet. He had hard hard hands, shiny black hair and a whisky bottle down between his feet. Elvis. His car looked exactly like that old Roxy red Capri. We used to drive it out along the stream. Rhonda Ford would sit and wait on all the stones and all the dirt. (She loved him too.) With her bare C. underneath her skirt. Putting on lipstick. She loved lipstick. She stole me some for my birthday. 'Smile babe,' she said, shoving it at me. 'You're so pretty if you keep smiling.' I was bursting with happiness as I put my mouth to the bottle. He revved up the motor. A wasp buzzed in my ear. The sound reverberated down the street.

The kid and I took a sharp left and drove by the daffodils. (In the April field.)

An orteil in the soup

You could see the swelling river slipping between the corrugated ice banks. The boys were leaned against the restaurant windows. (Glen Miller, Gourmet, said the sign.) Watching the houses heave up in a tumbled line. Walls wrench'd wider apart all the time. By the burgeoning iceblocks. 'Fuck!' said one. The cold air moved closer. The old red Capri sped right by the short shorts. The kid snuggled up on the car seat. Her feet were wet. Keep moving. We cut through the heavenly blue dusk. My nostrils smarted for something warm and velvety. Like the small scented Ps in the centrefold of flowers. We decided to take refuge up the ramp behind the Bargain Basement.

'Twas the snake woman that scared us. She was in this ad for a strip show. Flashing on the glass wall. Her black leather suit didn't save her from the whip. Kept coming back when someone flicked the switch. And hitting her in the face. Suddenly the kid sprang out and ran. She's all I've got so I ran after her. She disappeared around the Rond Point. I couldn't get down the ramp. Two dykes reached out a hand. 'Pretend we're three,' I whispered (sneaking a look over my shoulder at the snake woman). 'Then we'll be free.' I don't know why I said that. It was a stupid thing to say. I saw the kid crying on the other side of the street.

Wine on the windows

I was pretty petrified to try the razorblade trick. She made it sound so simple. You stick the blade deep in your mitt. Leaving only the little purple point free. Then you go down to the Bargain Basement. Best because they don't have those computerized tags that click as you sneak things into your bag. The stuff's too cheap. So when nobody's looking you just slice off the nice unprogrammed label and stick the spoils under your sweater. Or someplace. Scott-free. What a trip. Except nobody said what to do with the ticket. Just leave it there? Telltale traces. Dirty notes under the raspberry bushes. When the snow melts. I don't know nothin' about them. Honest Mom. Then she didn't know if she should say what was inside. Uh Did those boys ever? Keep smiling. Nice girls always smile. We walk the line our arms wide open all the time.

So you can't see

Arm 'n arm the kid and I strolled into the Bargain Basement. I had the blade deep in my mitt. Which was green. For the girl with green eyes. (She used to give those looks.) We went by a shattered glass terrasse. To Bathurst's B.B., said the sign. People sat shivering (for it was like November). The basement was done all up in an Easter extravaganza. For the Springtime / Au Printemps Bonanza. Softest nosegays of nylon nighties and pastel panties. The kid went wild. Up and down the aisle. Caressing the nylons. Burying her nose in the negligées. I readied my razorblade. Looked over my shoulder. Strange. No one in sight. I got scared. 'Let's get outta here,' I said. Then we saw it. Realer than real. Layer upon layer of sublime silken petals. Ever more scarlatly toward the centrefolds. Luminations of swollen lumps out of which peeped the tiny little points of sparkling Ps. Spreading strange perfume. Lording it over the place like the crown jewels. (Must have been some new sort of technology.) The sun shining on it like a halo. 'Oh Mommy,' said the kid. 'Let's go,' I said.

Speak to the busboy

If only the spring would come. Everything's got all swollen up. Points in the embonpoint. The kid and I snuggled up tight. Very very easy to be true (since that old Capri cruised off) in the empty night. We fell asleep. The unemployment cheque was running down the river. (I almost forgot.) No credit said the corner grocer piling his cans high on the counter. A red barrier. Hiding. Like the Capri guy (so he couldn't see the stomach bulge). No steak, spaghetti, even liver. Go fishing. He laughed hard. A cold wind came. It was the Portuguese demonstration*. (Tho' I didn't know it at the time.) 'Castrate all queers,' called the crowd. A kid in full flower stood slowly up in a bleeding coffin. Youth Snuffed By Faggot said the sign (In Back Shed). Men marched by in rainbow blouses. Faces covered by bright crosses. They were crying. A singing robin outside woke us up. The sun shining on its breast made it as red as that old convertible Capri.

Smile Babe

We got dressed and went out. The funny demonstration was still going by. Men wrapped in long black robes. A wide space was between them. They were silent. One stopped and stared. Surprising me as I slid the shiny pennies out of Sister Marilyn's milk bottle. A pretty-shaped bottle. 'Let's go,' I said to the kid. We got in the car. And started down the driveway. He tried to stop us. I stepped on it and nearly steamrollered him. He pointed at me as we roared off. 'Lesbian,' he screamed.

We kept moving. In the April field a fist was clutched. (Daffodils from the last feminist demo.) The red spot rose in the rearview. That old Roxy red Capri came closer. He had his eye beaded on the short shorts. His body swayed to the rock beat on the radio. The seat rocked.

We stopped at a wool shop. The kid was weaving a lampshade. Bangles, spangles and white shiny things. We stopped at the door, seeing someone I sort of knew. 'Have to do something about those Portuguese,' I said. I don't know why I said that. It was a silly thing to say. 'Yeah; she said. 'They're after my sister, too.' 'Who's your sister?' 'S.,' she said. Then I got really scared. S. was the girl with the green eyes.

We got in the car. A cold wind was coming up. Oh thank God it started. You could see the demo way down the street. 'I'm-the-quite-empty,' I said to the kid. She snuggled closer despite the hole in the floor. Some flowers would be nice. Little sparkling Ps. I could see my lips sinking between the silken velvet petals in search of the strange perfume, of the sunlight flashing like fish beneath the pond's surface. Bright as the teeth of the girl with the green eyes.

The sliding red spot. Smile Babe

We decided to go to the Bargain Basement. To have another look at the Easter Extravaganza. To cheer us up. The glass terrasse was deserted. But the Portuguese were coming. We disappeared down the stairs. There it stood in the Easter sunlight. Purple-rose. Softer than my grandmother's satin slips. I let the petals slide between my fingers. Squeezing slightly. My nose entered the embonpoint. The perfume. I looked over my shoulder. I could see nobody. 'Open your schoolbag,' I whispered. My mouth was dry. I slipped in the flowers. She smiled. We left quickly.

She was sitting on the back seat holding the flowers. When suddenly the red spot rose up again in the rearview. Before disappearing in the heavenly blue dust. I put my hand over the visor.

When I removed it the red spot was sliding back again. Coming closer and closer. The old Roxy red Capri. Out of the heavenly blue dust. It entered us from behind. You could see the baby boots on the dashboard. I smiled. The blood ran down my teeth.

The blue-suited security men surrounded my car. The kid was crying on the corrugated ice bank. They took me and took my flowers. I was locked in a place by a parking lot. My lips have swollen so, my tongue is like a point in the embonpoint. There's a torn patch in the sky. If only I could smell some Fs. Maybe the spring would come back.

PLUS TWO

BOTTOMS UP

Montréal, Quebec: I return to the site of an old novel. This will not always be a street of failure, even if still playing the former glamour of the seedy. French-language covers of country music are playing on the radio. Men (sit) alone at tables. One with haggard bearded face. His lower jaw (is) toothless. Teeth in dreams = sex. The low façades opposite parading peeling tin cornices. An air of stagnation possibly verging on cliché. I take some verbs out; put them in again.

It is the hottest summer ever. Meteorologists are, with divine hindsight, admitting global warming. To escape the heat, I go to a dark afternoon theatre. Where a sassy high school troupe's performing Büchner's *Wozeck*. The adolescents' sweet songs juxtaposed on the gloom and violence under, somehow dissolving earlier-decade interpretations foregrounding worn-out existential despair.

Crossing a parking lot behind a smoked meat shop, I am thinking a story, to avoid eternally returning (to keep it moving), might be structured thus: an 'older' woman writer circulates at a 'fringe' theatre festival of young artists. She has lost her love. Feels discombobulated. Nothing. She skirts the crowd asking several twenty-year-olds: anything good? She will then string a humiliated (but raunchy) love tale together, interlaying bits of youthful sweetness and anger, representing to her in her present state of emptiness, a more contemporaneously rapid conflation of beginnings and endings. A word about narrative:

At another table, a man shakes his purple-shirted shoulders in the hot bar air. To 'Caught With Your Pants Down.' Drinking straight tequila. The same table where C. and I sat. Discussing why our favourite writers of 'new' (experimental) narrative are not rich and famous. 'Too abject?' she ventures. In a bag at our feet, some cheaply extravagant dollhouse boudoir furniture purchased for her little son. From the store with the saggy awning opposite. Leaving, we forget it. Outside another man passing. With several teeth missing. Teeth = action. But why the narrator (the woman) endlessly remarking. Such toothless ghosts of subjects. Among dozens of better-furbished faces? Is her 'local' constructed out of some kind of distancing or bias? Or 'mere' projection of love's losses? I am thinking not abject the subject. Unless negatively framed at point of conjunction between work and the world. When site's signed minor (inadequate). And exterior = dominant. Yet, intrinsic and extrinsic syntax are not separate; rapidly they mate.* Should I be happy the lover having sex with no one? If having only virtual sex with me? I take some verbs out. And put them in again. A word about the waitress:

Dominatrix in clinging leopard-spotted polyester. Small breasts. Ponytail. Fortyish. Saying (in québécois): UN verre de vin-maison ne te fera pas de mal, one glass of house wine will not ruin the stomach. I.e. it's terrible. For 7 5 cents more you can have a quarter litre. Adding: you look en forme, terrific. We tell each other – in guise of complimenting – we haven't changed in years. I opting for the smallest quantity of red vinegar. Now young woman passing by window. Huge breasts encased in tight halter top. Some little cap over short hair. And – upper incisors gone. Like the meteorologist, I admitting only to coincidence of circumstances. Projecting accu-mulated lack on unsuspecting bodies. (Waitress bringing unasked for quarter litre.) Which bodies, in being thus sentenced, already frozen in past gesture or alias. While environment drifting else-where. As in that restless white river lover wanting to attack with kayak. Drifting eternally toward full-colour horizons. The silver flashes indicating minor notes of salmon struggling upstream. Sitting close beside her, I ironically allowing such tergiversation, such battering by context, likely ideal posture for contemporane-ous narrating. Just as lover putting hand under skirt cut on the bias to flare out attractively at the bottom. And saying she still wanting something with 'us.' A story is something you can put your teeth into:

But what might happen here? With (soon) a closed sign across the window. Two blocks down. A polished glass and marble multi-storey, multi-venue, multi-media repertory theatre. Having replaced the crushed blue façade of the smoky cozy café-cinéma where we used to see old or experimental European movies. Built by québécois Soft Image inventor Daniel Langlois. We're like that here: always oscillating between the ultra-modern and the crum-bling. The sound system's so efficient, one feels, watching the

Buena Vista Social Club, as if in some club in crumbling Havana. Though the octogenarian musicians having mostly ceased performing on their blockaded island. Because 'nowhere' to go. Until Ry Cooder choreographing their (global) return. I am thinking of when Québec liberationists claiming solidarity with Cuba. Which solidarity currently updated to meaning 'corporate opportunity.' At last, the Cubans playing Carnegie Hall. I am thinking how narrative, if fronted, marketed from economically preferential geographical site, though being troped as exotically remote, must (paradoxically) scale global walls or languish. I am thinking of Cuban sunsets, suffused toward evening with a little blood. Of the woman's eye growing humid, sentimental. When, in the movie, the elderly guitarist exclaiming: 'There is nothing like a night of love.' To keep it moving, I take some verbs out and put them in again. A word about identity:

Now the waitress in her leopardskin is leaning over the purple shirt. Who's reading a sexy men's magazine. Pausing, he pulls a huge fluorescent flashlight still wrapped in hard plastic cover from a bag. She points out (speaking [naturellement] French): it's no good without batteries. Laughing. I can smell him. The conversation seguing to European-French actress Catherine Deneuve. The waitress declaring in drawn-out North-American French diphthongs Deneuve 'plate,' boring: 'Always the same tone.' Outside a friend passing by window. Looking for a date. Very strong shoulders. Her long red hair streaming out behind. I know she has latex gloves in her bag. Walking naturally, she 'vogues.' Causing her to get thrown out of women's washrooms. For being 'wrong' gender. I am thinking how certain minor or unusual demeanors, if flaunted, getting read 'extrinsically' as unappealing or threatening. (In Canada, 'French' often = flamboyant or risqué;

coincidentally, same thing for 'queer'). This can be devastating. Or interesting. Friend passing again, very feminine in wrap-around skirt, curly red hair. Yet walking as if faking it. I am thinking how narrator (other). IF not knowing how friend herself-self-perceiving, able to create a relationship with reader permitting permutation of both obvious and unspeakable. The body being capable of gestures contrary to understanding. I am thinking of narrative as sub-stantive. Generated precisely at point of disso-nance. By even-ing out subject/object weight at each end of sentence. A word about affect:

[It has never occurred to me to be a poet. The poet, even when 'absent,' rests imbricated in her utter façade of language. While the reader happily at play. In her sandbox of spaces. Lacking spon-taneity, I am drawn to the violence of animation. Experienced by a subject. Drifting toward object. Across the placement of the verb. Which nakedness, exposure, seeming somehow progressive, egal-itarian. Yet failing to make the woman (narrator) cease obsession with beginnings (causes) and endings (conclusions). So trauma still risking terminating in single unbearable seduction scene. I am thinking of certain literary feminists. Who using devices copped from poetry to construct porous or unbounded subject, capable of merging somewhat ecologically with context. I am thinking of the gap of the unspeakable. There may be no animal boundary – just the stream and the pleasure that lies in it, teasing the poet.* I am thinking about the portentousness of sentencing. Alternately (defensively?), I am thinking that a sentence in a community of sentences (paragraphs) somehow leaving impression of consciously reaching out in communicative gesture. Notwithstanding characteristic narrative flick of head back over shoulder. At point of the period. For purpose of getting ...

bearings. This I finding … touching. A word about the geography
of the bar]:

Many empty tables. Two beefs in dark corner. Chairs fading
outward. Toward sunwashed waitress, purple shirt and harsh light
of street. Waitress, flashlight and me. A sign above our heads: 'Les
crevettes de MATANE arrivées!!! Fraîches. MATANE shrimp
in!!!! Fresh.' The drawn-out québécois fraîîîches savorously feminine and plural. The waitress and purple shirt still complaining
Deneuve lacking edge. Offering as replacement québécoise country music star. Recently coming out with 'fabulous CD.' Though
'star' still having to work nightly in bars. Very tough if you're
pregnant. Outside, young nomad in artfully torn outfit and fifty-
dollar-haircut. Asking for change in anglicized French. They come
here from the suburbs. Not to feel guilty. In this huge dark room
with stuffed animals on walls, I am thinking of simulation in a
diminishing French-speaking city, where everyone considering
themselves minority; yet in some way also faking it. I am thinking
of consequence for narrative, so often straining toward 'natural'
on site where continental popular culture in perpetual transmi-
gration from Germanic to Latinate. Of Mickey Mouse, Patsy
Klein, Sylvester Stallone, moving lips in English. While saying
something else entirely. I am thinking of living on a Renaissance
Ponte Vecchio: less bridge between than Babel of echoes.* Whose
interpretation requiring, precisely, resistance to meaning. I am
thinking of narration as introjection. Many relatives have
dentures. A word about hybridity:

Two blocks up. Little stages. Blue-and-white fleur-de-lys flags for
the fête nationale. The Argentinean tango I missed. Somehow
having erased Québec 'patron' Saint Jean Baptiste's bleeding and

miserable little lamb. Featured in earlier decades' national feast-day celebrations.** Fête progressing north. Group doing samba. Québécois folk songs. Block production of Molière farce. Free good food. Everyone speaking 'with accent.' Whole family dragging mahogany dining table out on sidewalk. Now eating supper. Later, I, sleepless, listening to thunderclaps on John Cage piece. To compensate for dryness. Leopardskin waitress offering another glass of vinegar. Muscled guy in tight sleeveless t-shirt and gleaming chain with cross. I am thinking of narrative as opaque barrier. There is no limit between life and deathly fascination. Viva Che! on wall. Now I must go before another cigarette. Buy food. Take messages. If any. The disease is not under control. Police car outside.

Notes

The Virgin Denotes

p. 10 Young journalists know what to write not to get spiked, and know even better when freedom of speech is restricted. In the atmosphere that reigned following invocation of the War Measures Act, it seemed for a time risky to link social aspects of the manifesto (such as terrible unemployment and working conditions) to the crisis, although assumption of such a relationship seemed implicit for progressive journalists prior to the Act. Interestingly, a month after the WMA was invoked, the professional journalists' association was calling for a provincial inquiry into freedom of the press, claiming that government pressure was leading to both censorship and self-censorship.

Withdrawal

p. 59 'Rang': French for concession road.

Petty Thievery

p. 78 At the time of writing of this story, a teenager, son of Portuguese immigrants, had been murdered in Toronto. Two gay men were charged with the crime and tension between individuals in the two communities increased. There was a virulent anti-gay demo, organized by members of the Portuguese community, herein fictionalized.

Bottoms Up

'Bottoms Up' was published online at *Narrativity*: http://www. sfsu.edu/~newlit/narrativity/issueone.html

The piece is in dialogue with Carla Harryman and with Robert Glück, Camille Roy, Dianne Chisholm, Sarah Schulman and others.

*Textual references (pages 84, 87, 88) are respectively to Barrett Watten's *Total Syntax*; to a cover citation from *Sight* by Lyn Hejinian and Leslie Scalapino, and to Sherry Simon's essay 'The Paris Arcades, the Ponte Vecchio, and the Comma of Translation.'

**Saint Jean Baptiste Day, June 24, is a national feast day in Québec.

Acknowledgements

Thanks to Bruce Russell for the cover image and much thanks to Alana Wilcox for editing suggestions on the new work and for the inside design, and to Darren Wershler-Henry for the cover design. I'd also like to express my gratitude to Frank Davey as original editor of this book and to Stan Bevington and all the people who have kept Coach House alive.

ABOUT THE AUTHOR

Gail Scott's six books include *My Paris* (listed among *Quill and Quire*'s top ten in 1999), *Main Brides*, the popular novel *Heroine*, and the essay collection *Spaces like Stairs*. Her translation of Michael Delisle's novel *Le Désarroi du matelot* (*The Sailor's Disquiet*), was short-listed for the Governor General's Award for literary translation in 2001. A former journalist and founding editor of the periodicals *Spirale* and *Tessera*, she is currently a co-editor of *Narrativity*, a web magazine devoted to the subject of new narrative, out of the Poetry Center at San Francisco State University. She lives in Montréal.

Typeset in Sabon and Vintage. Printed and bound at Coach House Printing on bpNichol Lane, 2002.

Edited and designed by Alana Wilcox
Cover design by Darren Wershler-Henry
Author photo by Jean-François Bérubé
The cover image is a tourist postcard of Montréal from the 1940s

Read the online version of this text on our website:
www.chbooks.com

Send a request to be included on our e-mailing list:
mail@chbooks.com

Call us toll-free:
1 800 367 6360

Coach House Books
401 Huron Street on bpNichol Lane
Toronto ON
M5S 2G5